AF584310

Somewhere in Australia

Dedicated to my late nephew, Michael Gismondi,
and to my wonderful partner, Lara Jefferson,
and our two sons, Ryan and Aiden—M.P.

For Emily—D.S.

Scholastic Australia
An imprint of Scholastic Australia Pty Limited
PO Box 579 Gosford NSW 2250
ABN 11 000 614 577
www.scholastic.com.au

Part of the Scholastic Group
Sydney • Auckland • New York • Toronto • London • Mexico City
• New Delhi • Hong Kong • Buenos Aires • Puerto Rico

First published by Scholastic Australia in 2013.
This edition published in 2023.

A catalogue record for this book is available from the National Library of Australia

ISBN: 978-1-76129-744-1

Typeset in Old Claude.

Printed in China by RR Donnelley.

Scholastic Australia's policy, in association with its printers, is to use papers that are renewable and made efficiently from wood from responsibly managed sources, so as to minimise its environmental footprint.

10 9 8 7 6 5 4 3 25 26 27 28 29 / 2

Somewhere in Australia

MARCELLO PENNACCHIO

Illustrated by DANNY SNELL

A Scholastic Australia Book

Somewhere in Australia, in a land of scorching sun,
lived a mother kangaroo and her little joey one.

'Hop,' said the mother. 'I hop,' said the one,
as they hopped over land scorched by the hot sun.

In the centre of Australia, near a place called Uluru,
lived a mother kookaburra and her little chicks two.

'Laugh,' said the mother. 'We laugh,' said the two,
as they laughed and they flew over a rock called Uluru.

On the east coast of Australia, in a river flowing out to sea, lived a mother platypus and her platy-pups three.

'Swim,' said the mother. 'We swim,' said the three, as they swam in a river that flowed out to the sea.

In Australia's 'Apple Isle', on a rainforest floor,
lived a mother Tassie devil and her little devils four.

'Growl,' said the mother. 'We growl,' said the four,
as they growled and they foraged on a rainforest floor.

On the mainland of Australia, where gum trees grow and thrive, lived a mother dingo and her dingo pups five.

'Howl,' said the mother. 'We howl,' said the five,
as they howled and they played where gum trees grow and thrive.

At the top end of Australia, in a land of spinifex,
lived a mother death adder and her little snakes six.

'Slither,' said the mother. 'We slither,' said the six,
as they slithered and they hid in among the spinifex.

In the outback of Australia, where nothing much is livin',
sat a mother thorny devil and her little lizards seven.

'Bask,' said the mother. 'We bask,' said the seven,
as they basked and they sunned where nothing much is livin'.

In the Blue Mountains of Australia, near a Wollemi pine,
lived a mother green frog and her little froglets nine.

'Jump,' said the mother. 'We jump,' said the nine,
as they jumped and they leaped near a Wollemi pine.

Along Australia's southern shores, on a wattle tree stem,
lived a mother red-back spider and her little spiders ten.

'Hunt,' said the mother. 'We hunt,' said the ten,
as they hunted for their quarry on a wattle tree stem.

All across Australia, in the dreams of little sleepy ones,
Are sand and sea, bush and desert, the land of the scorching sun.